Just For You,
Blue Kangaroo!

Emma Chichester Clark

A

Andersen Press
LONDON

For Eliza

Copyright © 2004 by Emma Chichester Clark
The rights of Emma Chichester Clark to be identified as the author and illustrator
of this work have been asserted by her in accordance with the Copyright, Designs and Patents Act, 1988.
First published in Great Britain in 2004 by Andersen Press Ltd., 20 Vauxhall Bridge Road, London SW1V 2SA.
Published in Australia by Random House Australia Pty., 20 Alfred Street, Milsons Point, Sydney, NSW 2061.
All rights reserved. Colour separated in Switzerland by Photolitho AG, Zürich.
Printed and bound in Italy by Grafiche AZ, Verona.

10   9   8   7   6   5   4   3   2   1

British Library Cataloguing in Publication Data available.

ISBN 1 84270 322 6
This book has been printed on acid-free paper

Blue Kangaroo belonged to Lily.
He was her very own kangaroo,
and it was his first Christmas.
"Look!" whispered Lily. "It's snowing –
just for you, Blue Kangaroo!"

Lily made her own Christmas cards.
She drew robins and holly and she stuck stars on them.

"I've made one for everyone," she said,
"and one just for you, Blue Kangaroo!"

"Just for me!"
thought Blue Kangaroo.
"I wish I could make one
for Lily."

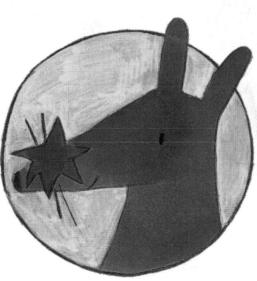

The next day, Lily and her mother made Christmas decorations. They cut up coloured paper and stuck it with glue.

"It's going to be so pretty!" cried Lily. "And it's just for you, Blue Kangaroo!"

"And for *you*," said her mother.

In the afternoon, Uncle George and Lily's father
brought home the Christmas tree.
"It's Blue Kangaroo's first Christmas, Uncle George!"
said Lily.

"Well then," said Uncle George, "here's a tree just for you, Blue Kangaroo!"

"Just for me?"
thought Blue Kangaroo.
"What will I do with a tree?"

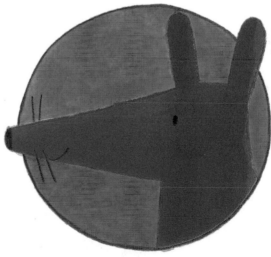

The next day, Lily and her mother wrapped up presents.
"I hope you're not looking, because this one's just for you,
Blue Kangaroo," said Lily.

Lily helped to put the presents under
the tree.

"Just for me!"
thought Blue Kangaroo.
"I wish I had one for Lily."

Later on, Aunt Jemima and Aunt Florence came.
Aunt Jemima brought mince pies and Aunt Florence
brought gingerbread men.

"One for you, Lily, one for your little brother . . .
and this one is just for you, Blue Kangaroo!"
said Aunt Florence.

"Just for me,"
thought Blue Kangaroo.
"It's just *like* me!"

Lily's grandparents arrived in the evening.
"It's Blue Kangaroo's first Christmas!"
said Lily.

Everyone sang carols around the tree, and then Lily sang
one all by herself. "Just for you,
Blue Kangaroo!" she said.

"Just for me!"
thought Blue Kangaroo.
"I wish I could sing for Lily."

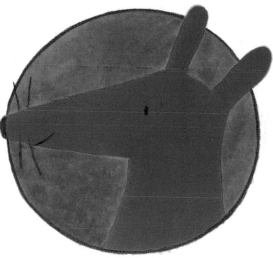

Before bed, Lily hung up her stocking.
"Do you think Father Christmas will come?" she asked.
"He'll come when you are fast asleep," said her mother.

"Good night, Blue Kangaroo," whispered Lily,
and she closed her eyes tight . . .

. . . but Blue Kangaroo
lay wide-eyed through
the night.

Suddenly, there was a funny noise.
Blue Kangaroo's whiskers bristled. His ears tingled.
"Is it Father Christmas?" he wondered.

A big yellow moon was shining through the house
and everything was quiet.
Then he heard it again . . .

"It *must* be Father Christmas!" thought Blue Kangaroo.
"Perhaps he can help me."
Blue Kangaroo waited. The noises got louder . . .
then crashing, and BUMP!
"Father Christmas?" he whispered.

"What can I do for you, little Blue Kangaroo?"
asked Father Christmas.
"Well, Lily says everything is just for me but I want
something just for *her*, and I haven't got anything,"
said Blue Kangaroo sadly.

"Has she been good?" asked Father Christmas.
"Oh, yes!" said Blue Kangaroo.
"Then you might just find something in my sack,"
said Father Christmas. "Have a look." Blue Kangaroo looked,
and he found something just *exactly* right.

Father Christmas wrote a label for Blue Kangaroo,
so that he could hang his present on the tree.
Then they had some milk and cookies.

"Good night, Blue Kangaroo," said Father Christmas.
"Lily is a lucky girl to have such a good kangaroo as you!"

In the morning, Lily ran downstairs with Blue Kangaroo.

She found that there were *three* stockings hanging on the mantelpiece!

"Look!" said Lily. "It says, 'Just for you, my good friend Blue Kangaroo, from Father Christmas.' How did that happen?" she asked.

Then Lily noticed something else.
"Look!" she said. "A little blue heart on the Christmas tree!
That wasn't there yesterday! Who can it be for?"

The little blue heart had a ribbon with
a tiny Christmas card tied onto it.
Lily read the message out loud. It said:
Just for you, Lily.
With love from Blue Kangaroo.
"Oh, Blue Kangaroo," whispered Lily,
hugging him tight. "Just for me, from you!"
"Yes," thought Blue Kangaroo happily.
"Just for you, Lily. Just for you!"